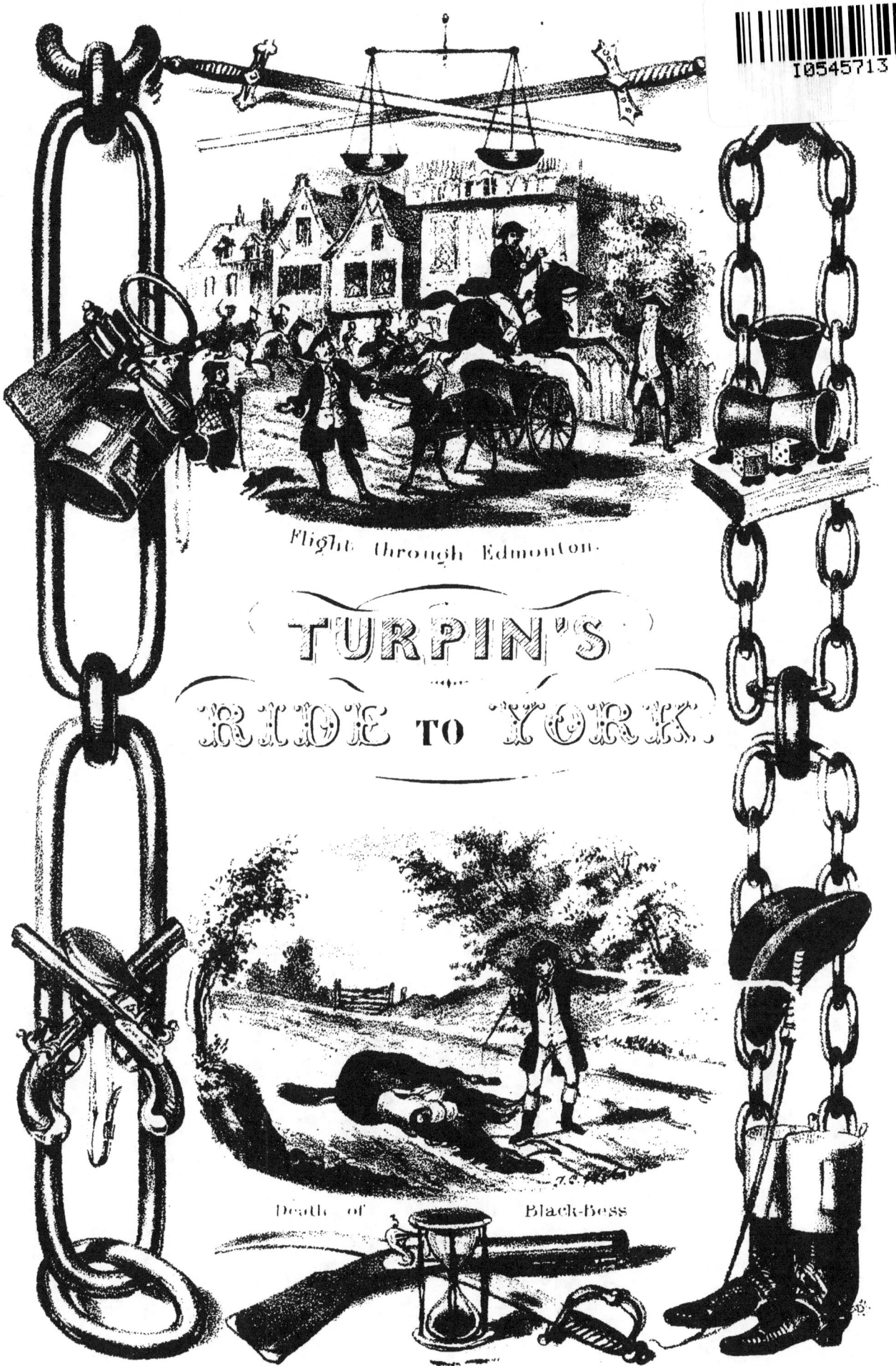

Flight through Edmonton.

TURPIN'S
RIDE TO YORK.

Death of Black-Bess

Published by E. Glover, Water Lane, Fleet St.
W. Clerk, Lith., 202 High Holborn.

THE ILLUSTRATED LIBRARY OF ROMANCE.

PART I.

TURPIN'S

RIDE TO YORK.

Then one halloo, boys! one loud cheering halloo!
To the swiftest of coursers—the gallant, the true;
For the sportsman unborn shall the memory bless
Of the horse of the highwayman—bonny BLACK BESS.

LONDON:

GLOVER, PUBLISHER.

1839.

J. CUNNINGHAM, PRINTER, CROWN-COURT, FLEET-STREET.

TURPIN'S RIDE TO YORK.

CHAPTER I.

THE RENDEZVOUS AT KILBURN.

Hind. Drink deep, my brave boys, of the bastinado,
Of stramazons, tinctures, and slic passatas;
Of the carricado, and rare embrocado,
Of blades, and rapier hilts of surest guard,
Of the Vincentio and Burgundian ward.
Have we not bravely tossed this bombast foil button?
Win gold and wear gold boys, 'tis we that merit it.
                    PRINCE OF PRIGS' REVELS.

THE present straggling suburb, known as Kilburn, had scarcely
been called into existence a century ago, and an inn, with a few
detached farm-houses, were the sole habitations to be found in the
present populous vicinage. The place of refreshment for the ruralizing
cockney of 1737 was an ancient substantial-looking tenement of the good
old stamp, with great bay windows, and a balcony in front, bearing as
its ensign the jovial visage of the lusty knight, Jack Falstaff. Shaded
by a spreading elm, stood a circular bench, embracing the aged trunk of
the tree; sufficiently tempting, no doubt, to incline the wanderer on
those dusty ways to "rest and be thankful," and to cry *encore* to a
frothing tankard of the best ale to be obtained within the chimes of Bow
Bells.

At the left of a table was seated, or rather lounged, a slender, elegant-
looking young man, with dark languid eyes, sallow complexion, and
features wearing that peculiarly pensive expression which, we regret to
say, is sometimes found more pleasing than it ought to be in the eyes of
the gentle sex. Habited in a light summer riding dress, fashioned according to the taste of the time, but of plain and unpretending material,
and rather under than over dressed, he had, perhaps, on that very
account, perfectly the air of a gentleman. There was, altogether, an
absence of pretension about him, which, combined with great apparent

self-possession, contrasted very forcibly with the vulgar assurance of his showy companions. The figure of the youth was slight, even to fragility, giving little outward manifestation of the vigour of frame he in reality possessed. To save the reader any speculation as to who this spark might be, we will at once acquaint him with his name and calling. He was a no less distinguished personage than Tom King, a noted Tobyman of his time, who obtained, from his appearance and address, the *sobriquet* of the " Gentleman Highwayman."

His acquaintance with Turpin was singular, and originated in a *rencontre*. Struck with his appearance, Dick presented a pistol, and bade King deliver. The latter burst into a laugh, and an explanation ensued. Thenceforward they became sworn brothers—the Pylades and Orestes of the Road; and though seldom seen together in public, had many a merry moonlight ride in company.

Next to King sat one Jerry Juniper; a character well known at the time, as a constant frequenter of all races, fairs, regattas, ship-launches, bull-baits, and prize-fights.

One guest alone remains, and him we shall briefly dismiss. The reader, we imagine, will scarcely need to be told who was the owner of those keen, grey eyes—those exuberant red whiskers—that airy azure frock. It was

> Our brave co-partner of the Roads,
> Skilful surveyor of highways and hedges;

in a word—Dick Turpin ! He was a good-humoured, good-looking man, with immense bushy, red whiskers, a freckled, florid complexion, sandy hair, rather inclined to scantiness towards the scalp of the head, and garnishing the nape of his neck with a ruff of crisp little curls, like the ring on a monk's shaven crown. Notwithstanding this tendency to baldness, Dick could not be more than thirty, though his looks were some five years in advance. His face was one of those inexplicable countenances, which appear to be proper to a peculiar class of men— a regular Newmarket physiognomy—compounded chiefly of cunning and assurance—not low cunning, nor vulgar assurance, but crafty sporting subtlety, careless as to results—indifferent to obstacles—ever on the alert for the main chance—game and turf all over— eager, yet easy— keen, yet quiet. He was somewhat showily dressed, in such mode that he looked half like a fine gentleman of that day, half like a jockey of our own—his nether man appeared in well-fitting, well-worn buckskins, and boots with tops, not unconscious of the saddle; while the airy extravagance of his broad-skirted sky-blue riding coat, the richness of his vest, the pockets of which were beautifully exuberant, according to the mode of 1737; the smart luxuriance of his shirt frill, and a certain curious taste in the size and style of his buttons, proclaimed that, in his own esteem at least, his person did not appear altogether unworthy of decoration : nor, in justice to Dick, can we allow that he was in error. He was a model of a man for five feet ten; square, compact, capitally built in every particular, excepting that his legs were slightly embowed, which defect probably arose from his being almost constantly on horseback—a sort of exercise in which Dick greatly delighted, and was accounted a superb rider.

Dick had been called upon to act as president of the board, and an excellent president he made, sedulously devoting himself to the due administration of the punch bowl. Not a rummer was allowed to stand empty for an instant. Toast, sentiment, and anacreontic song, succeeded each other at speedy intervals; but there was no speechifying—no politics. He left church and state to take care of themselves. Whatever his politics might be, Dick never allowed them to interfere with his pleasures. His maxim was to make the most of the passing moment; the *dum vivimus vivamus* was never out of his mind; a precautionary measure which we recommend to the adoption of all gentlemen of the like, or any other precarious profession.

Notwithstanding all Dick's efforts to promote conviviality, seconded by the excellence of the beverage itself, conversation, somehow or other, began to flag; from being general it became particular. Tom King, who was no punch-bibber, especially at that time of day, fell into a deep reverie—your gamesters often do so—while the Magus, who had smoked himself drowsy, was composing himself to a doze. Turpin seized this opportunity of addressing a few words on matters of business to Jerry Juniper, or, as he now chose to be called, Count Conyers, in which the treachery of Jerry's mistress called forth many imprecations on the sex, which to Tom King, whose abstraction did not prevent him catching part of their conversation, appeared little short of blasphemous, and arousing from his tooth-pick reverie he exclaimed, " Peace, base calumniators, I say. None shall dare to abuse that dear devoted sex in the hearing of their champion, without pricking a lance with me in their behalf. What do you, either of you, who abuse woman in that wholesale style, know of her? Nothing—less than nothing; and yet you venture, upon your paltry experience, to lift up your voices and decry the sex. Now, I *do* know her—and upon my own experience, I avouch, that as a sex, woman, compared with man, is as an angel to a devil. As a sex, woman is faithful—loving—self-sacrificing. *We* 'tis that make her otherwise; *we*, selfish, exacting, neglectful men; we teach her indifference, and then blame her apt scholarship. We spoil our own hand, and then blame the cards. No abuse of women in my hearing. Give me a glass of grog, Dick—the sex!—three times three.

" Well," replied Dick, replenishing King's rummer, while he laughed heartily, " I shan't refuse your toast, though my heart don't respond to your sentiments. Ah, Tom! the sex you praise so much will, I fear, prove your undoing. Do as you please, but curse me if ever I pin my life to a petticoat."

" Well," said King, " all you can say don't alter my good opinion of the women.   Not a secret have I from the girl of my heart.   She could have sold me over and over again, if she had chosen—but my sweet Sue is not the wench to do that."

"It is not too late," said Dick.   "Your Dalilah may yet hand you over to the Philistines."

"Then I shall die in a good cause," said King: but

> The Tyburn tree
> Has no terrors for me,
> Let better men swing—I'm at liberty.

I shall never come to the scragging post, unless you turn topsman, Dick Turpin.   My nativity has been cast, and the stars have declared that I am to die by the hand of my best friend—and that's you—eh, Dick ?"

"It sounds like it," replied Turpin; "but I advise you not to become too intimate with Jack Ketch—he may prove your best friend after all."

"Why faith, that's true," replied King, laughing: "and if I must ride backwards up Holborn-hill, I'll do the thing in good style, and honest Jack Ketch shall never want his dues.   A man should always die game. We none of us know how soon our turn may come, but come when it will, I shall never flinch from it—

> As the Highwayman's life is the fullest of zest,
> So the Highwayman's death is the briefest and best;
> He dies not as other men die, by degrees,
> But *at once!* without flinching—and quite at his ease—

as the song you are so fond of says.   When I die it will be of consumption.   And if the surgeon's knife must come near me, it will be after death.   There's some comfort in that reflection, at all events."

"True," replied Turpin, "and, with a little alteration, my song would suit you capitally—

> There is not a king, should you search the world round,
> So blithe as the king's king, Tom King, to be found:
> Dear woman's his empire, each girl is his own,
> And he'd have a long reign if he'd let them alone.

Ha! ha!"

"Ha! ha!" laughed Tom; "but now Dick, to change the subject. You are off, I understand, to Yorkshire to-night, Dick.   'Pon my soul, you are a wonderful fellow—an alibi personified!—here and every where at one and the same time—no wonder you are called the flying highway-man.   To-day in town—to-morrow at York—the day after at Chester. The devil only knows where you will pitch your quarters a week hence. There are rumours of you in all counties at the same moment.   This man swears you robbed him at Hounslow—that, on Salisbury plain—while another swears you monopolize Cheshire and Yorkshire, and that it isn't safe even to *hunt* without pops in your pocket.   I heard some devilish good stories of you at D'Osyndar's t'other day; the fellow who told them to me little thought that I was a brother blade."

"You flatter me," said Dick, smiling complacently, "but it's no merit of mine. Black Bess alone enables me to do it, and her's be the credit. Talking of being every where at the same time, you shall hear what she once did for me in Cheshire. Meantime a glass to the best mare in England—you won't refuse that toast, Tom. Ah! if your mistress was only as true to you as my nag to me, you might set at nought the tightest hempen cravat that was ever twisted, and defy your best friend to hurt you—Black Bess! and God bless her. And now for the song." Saying which, with much emotion, Turpin chaunted the following rhymes :—

BLACK BESS.

—————Illi ardua cervix,
Argutumque caput, brevis alvus, obesaque terga.
VIRGIL'S GEORGICS.

Let the lover his mistress's beauty rehearse,
And laud her attractions in languishing verse;
Be it mine in rude strains, but with *truth* to express,
The love that I bear to my bonny Black Bess.

From the West was her dam, from the East was her sire,
From the one came her swiftness, the other her fire;
No peer of the realm better blood can possess,
Than flows in the veins of my bonny Black Bess.

Look! look! how that eyeball glows bright as a brand!
That neck proudly arches, those nostrils expand!
Mark! that wide-flowing mane! of which each silky tress
Might adorn prouder beauties—though none like Black Bess.

Mark! that skin sleek as velvet, and dusky as night,
With its jet undisfigured by one lock of white;
The throat branched with veins, prompt to charge or caress,
Now, is she not beautiful?—bonny Black Bess!

Over highway and byway, in rough and smooth weather,
Some thousands of miles have we journeyed together;
Our couch the same straw, and our meal the same mess,
No couple more constant than I and Black Bess.

By moonlight, in darkness, by night, or by day,
Her headlong career there is nothing can stay;
She cares not for distance, she knows not distress,
Can you show me a courser to match with Black Bess!

Once it happened in Cheshire, near Dunham, I popped
On a horseman alone, whom I speedily stopped;
That I lightened his pockets you'll readily guess—
Quick work makes Dick Turpin when mounted on Bess.

Now it seems the man knew me; "Dick Turpin," said he,
"You shall swing for this job, as you live d'ye see:"
I laughed at his threats and his vows of redress,
I was sure of an *alibi* then with Black Bess.

The road was a hollow, a sunken ravine,
Overshadowed completely by wood like a screen;
I clambered the bank, and I needs must confess
That one touch of the spur grazed the side of Black Bess.

C

Brake, brook, meadow, and ploughed field, Bess fleetly bestrode,
As the crow wings her flight, we selected our road;
We arrived at Hough Green in five minutes or less—
My neck it was saved by the speed of Black Bess.

Stepping carelessly forward, I lounge on the green,
Taking excellent care that by all I am seen,
Some remarks on time's flight to the squires I address,
But I say not a word of the flight of Black Bess.

I mention the hour—it was just about four—
Play a rubber at bowls—think the danger is o'er;
When athwart my next game, like a checkmate at chess,
Comes the horseman in search of the rider of Bess.

What matter details?   Off with triumph I came,
He swears to the hour, and the squires swear the same;
I had robbed him at *four;* while at four *they* profess
I was quietly bowling—all thanks to Black Bess.

Then one halloo, boys! one loud cheering halloo!
To the swiftest of coursers, the gallant, the true!
For the sportsman unborn sha'll the memory bless,
Of the horse of the highwayman, bonny Black Bess.

Loud acclamations rewarded Dick's performance, and the party assumed once more a lively air; the glass was circulated so freely, that at last a final charge drained the ample bowl of its contents.

"The best of friends must part," said Dick, "and willingly would I order another whiff of punch, but that I think we have all had *enough to satisfy us,* as you milling coves have it, Zory! Your one eye has got a drop in it already, old fellow—and to speak the truth, I must be getting into the saddle without more delay, for I have a long ride before me. So now, pals, farewell!—a long farewell!" said Dick, in a tone of theatrical valediction; "and as I said before, the best friends must separate. We may soon meet again, or we now may part for ever. We cannot command our luck; but we can make the best of the span allotted to us. You have your game to play—I have mine; may each of us meet with the success he deserves."

"Egad I hope not," said King; "I am afraid in that case the chances would be against us."

"Well, then, the success we anticipate, if you like it better," rejoined Dick; "I have only to observe one thing more, namely, that I must insist upon being paymaster on the present occasion. Not a word—I won't hear a syllable. Landlord, I say—what, ho!" continued Dick, stepping out of the arbour, "here, my old Admiral of the White, what's the reckoning—what's to pay, I say?"

"Let ye know directly, sir," said mine host of the Falstaff.

"Order my horse—the black mare," added Dick.

"And mine," said King, "the sorrel colt. I'll ride with you a mile or two on the road, Dick; perhaps we may stumble upon something."

"Very likely."

"We meet at twelve, at D'Osyndar's, Jerry," said King, "if nothing happens."

Jerry nodded acquiescence; and while he went in search of the implements of the game of bowls Turpin, and King sauntered gently on the green.

It was a delicious evening. The sun was slowly declining, and glowed like a ball of fire amid the thick foliage of a neighbouring elm. Whether, like the robber, Tom King was touched by this glorious sunset, we pretend not to determine, but certain it was, that a shade of inexpressible melancholy passed across his handsome countenance, as he gazed in the direction of Harrow-on-the-Hill, which lying to the west of the green upon which they walked, stood out with its pointed spire and lofty college, against the ruddy sky. He spoke not—but Dick noticed the passing emotion.

"What ails you, Tom?" said he, with much kindness of manner, " are you not well, lad?"

"Yes, I am well enough," said King; "I know not what came over me, but looking at Harrow, I thought of my school days, and what I was *then*, and that bright prospect reminded me of my boyish hopes."

"Tut—tut," said Dick, " this is idle—you are a man now."

"I know I am," replied Tom, " but I *have* been a boy. Had I any faith in presentiments, I should say this is the last sunset I shall ever see."

"Here comes our host," said Dick, smiling, " I've no presentiment that that is the last bill I shall ever pay."

The bill was brought, and settled. As Turpin paid it, the man's conduct altogether was singular, and awakened Turpin's suspicions.

"Are our horses ready?" asked Dick quickly.

"They are, sir," said the landlord.

"Let us begone," whispered Dick to King; "I don't like this fellow's manner. I thought I heard a carriage draw up at the inn door just now—there may be danger. Be fly!" added he to Jerry and the Magus. "Now, sir," said he to the landlord, "lead the way. Keep on the alert, Tom." Dick's hint was not lost upon the two bowlers. They watched their comrades; and listened intently for any manifestation of alarm.

CHAPTER II.

A SURPRISE.

Was this well done, Jenny?
CAPTAIN MACHEATH.

WHILE Turpin and King are walking across the bowling-green, we shall see what has been passing outside the inn. Tom's presentiments of danger were not, it appeared, without foundation. Scarcely had the ostler brought forth our two Highwaymen's steeds, when a post-chaise, escorted by two or three horsemen, drove furiously up to the door. The sole occupant of the carriage was a lady, whose slight and pretty figure was all that could be distinguished of her, her face being closely veiled. The landlord, who was busied in casting up Turpin's account, rushed forth at the summons. A word or two passed between him and the horsemen, upon which the former's countenance fell. He posted in the direction of the garden; and the horsemen instantly dismounted.

"We have him now, sure enough," said one of them, a very small man, who looked, in his boots, like Buckle equipped for the Oaks.

"By the powers, I begin to think so," replied the other horseman; "but don't spoil all, Mr. Coates, by being too precipitate."

"Never fear that, Titus," said Coates; "he's sure to come for his mare. That's a *trap* certain to catch him, eh, Mr. Paterson. With the Chief Constable of Westminster to back us, the devil's in it if we are not a match for him."

"Take him quietly," said Paterson; "draw the chaise out of the way, lad. Take our tits to one side, and place their nags near the door ostler. Shall you be able to see him, ma'am, where you are?" asked the Chief Constable, walking to the carriage, and touching his hat to the lady within; and having received a satisfactory nod from the bonnet and veil, returned to his companions. "And now, gemmen," added he, "let's step aside a little. Don't use your fire-arms too soon."

As if conscious what was passing around her, and of the danger that awaited her master, Black Bess exhibited so much impatience, and plunged so violently, that it was with difficulty the ostler could hold her. "The devil's in the mare," said he, "what's the matter with her; she was quiet enough a few minutes since. So, ho! lass—stand."

Turpin and King meanwhile walked quickly through the house, preceded by the host, who conducted them, not without some inward trepidation, towards the door. Arrived there, each man rushed swiftly to his horse. Dick was in the saddle in an instant, and stamping her foot upon the ostler's leg, Black Bess compelled the man, yelling with pain, to quit his hold of the bridle. Tom King was not equally fortunate. Before he could mount his horse, a loud shout was raised, which startled the animal, and caused him to swerve, so that Tom lost his footing in the stirrup, and fell to the ground. He was instantly seized by Paterson, and a struggle commenced, King endeavouring, but in vain, to draw a pistol.

"Flip him, Dick—fire, or I'm taken," cried King. "Fire, damn you—why don't you fire?" shouted he in desperation, still struggling vehemently with Paterson, who was a strong man, and more than a match for such a light weight as King.

"I can't," cried Dick; "I shall hit you if I fire."

"Take your chance," shouted King, "is *this* your friendship?"

Thus urged, Turpin fired. The ball ripped up Paterson's coat, but did not wound him.

TURPINS RIDE TO YORK.   PLATE I.

Published by H Graves Water lane Fleet Street.

W.Clerk Lith. W. High Holborn.

" Again !" cried King; " shoot him, I say—don't you hear me? Fire again !"

Pressed as he was by foes on every side, himself their mark, for both Coates and Tyrconnel had fired upon him, and were now mounting their steeds to give chase, it was impossible that Turpin could take sure aim; add to which, in the struggle, Paterson and King were each moment changing their relative positions. He, however, would no longer hesitate, but again, at his friend's request, fired. The ball lodged itself in King's breast! He fell at once. At this instant a shriek was heard from the chaise : the window was thrown open, and her thick veil being drawn aside, the features of a very pretty female, now impressed with terror and contrition, were suddenly exhibited.

King fixed his glazing eyes upon her.

" Susan !" sighed he, " is it you that I behold?"

" Yes—yes, 'tis she, sure enough," said Paterson; " you see, ma'am, what you and such like have brought him to. However, you'll lose your reward; for he's going fast enough."

" Reward !" gasped King, " reward ! did she betray me?"

" Ay, ay, sir," said Paterson, " she blowed the gaff, if it's any consolation to you to know it."

" Consolation !" repeated the dying man; " perfidious !—oh !—the prophecy—my best friend—Turpin—I die by his hand." And vainly striving to raise himself, he fell backwards and expired. Alas! poor Tom !

" Mr. Paterson—Mr. Paterson !" cried Coates, " leave the landlord to look after the body of that dying ruffian, and mount with us in pursuit of the living rascal. Come, sir, quick, mount, dispatch. You see he is yonder; he seems to hesitate; we shall have him now."

" Well, gemmen, I'm ready," said Paterson; " but how the devil came you to let him escape you?"

" St. Patrick only knows," said Titus; " he's as slippery as an eel, and, like a cat, turn him which way you will, he is always sure to alight upon his legs. I would'nt wonder but we lose him now, after all, though he has such a small start; that mare flies like the wind."

" He shall have a tight run for it, at all events," said Paterson, putting spurs into his horse. " I've a good nag under me, and you are neither of you badly mounted; he is only three hundred yards before us, and the devil's in it if we can't run him down. It's a three hundred pound job, Mr. Coates, and well worth a race."

" You shall have another hundred from me, sir, if you take him," said Coates, urging his steed forward.

" Thank you, sir, thank you; follow my directions, and we'll make sure of him," said the Constable. " Gently, gently, not so fast up the hill; you see he's breathing his horse; all in good time, Mr. Coates, all in good time, sir."

And maintaining an equal distance, both parties cantered leisurely up, what we believe is now called the Windmill Hill. We shall now return to Turpin.

Aghast at the deed he had accidentally committed, Dick remained for a few moments irresolute; he perceived that King was mortally wounded, and that all attempts at rescue would be fruitless; he perceived, likewise, that Jerry had effected his escape from the bowling green, as he could detect his figure stealing along the hedge-side. He hesitated no longer. Turning his horse, he galloped slowly off, little heeding the pursuit with which he was threatened.

"Every bullet has its billet," said Dick, "but little did I think that I really should turn poor Tom's executioner. To the devil with this rascally snapper," cried he, throwing the pistol over the hedge. "I could never have used it again. 'Tis strange, too, that he should have foretold his own fate—devilish strange: and then that he should have been betrayed by the very blowen he trusted! that's a lesson, if I wanted any; but trust a woman! not I, the length of my little finger."

CHAPTER III.

THE HUE AND CRY.

Six gentlemen upon the road
  Thus seeing Gilpin fly,
With post-boy scampering in the rear,
  They raised the hue and cry :—

Stop thief! stop thief! a highwayman!
  Not one of them was mute;
And all and each that pass'd that way
  Did join in the pursuit.

JOHN GILPIN.

ARRIVED at the brow of the hill, whence such a beautiful view of the country surrounding the Metropolis is obtained, Turpin turned for an instant to reconnoitre his pursuers. Coates and Titus he utterly disregarded; but Paterson was a more formidable foe, and he well knew that he had to deal with a man of experience and resolution. It was then, for the first time, that the thoughts of executing his extraordinary ride to York first flashed across him; his bosom throbbed high with rapture, and he involuntarily exclaimed aloud, as he raised himself in the saddle, "By G—, I will do it!"

He took one last look at the great Babel that lay buried in a world of trees beneath him, and as his quick eye ranged over the magnificent prospect lit up by that gorgeous sunset, he could not help thinking of Tom King's last words. "Poor fellow!" thought Dick, "he said truly, he should never see another sunset." Aroused by the approaching clatter of his pursuers but little behind him, Dick struck into a lane

TURPIN'S RIDE TO YORK.

TURPIN'S FLIGHT THROUGH EDMONTON.

Published by E Gilbert, Water Lane, Fleet Street.

W. Clerk Lith, 202 High Holborn.

which lies on the right of the road, now called Shoot-up-hill Lane, and set off at a good pace in the direction of Hampstead.

"Now," cried Paterson, "put your tits to it, my boys; we must not lose sight of him for a second in these lanes."

And accordingly, as Turpin was by no means desirous of inconveniencing his mare in this early stage of the business, and as the ground was still upon an ascent, the parties still preserved their relative distances.

At length, after various twistings and turnings in that deep and devious lane; after scaring one or two farmers, and riding over a brood or two of ducks; dipping into the verdant valley of West End, and ascending another hill, Turpin burst upon the gorsy, sandy, and beautiful Heath of Hampstead; still shaping his course to the left, Dick made for the lower part of the heath, and skirted a path which leads towards North-End, passing the furze-crowned summit, which is at present crested by a clump of lofty pines.

It was here that the chase first assumed a character of interest. Being open ground, the pursued and pursuers were in full view of each other, and as Dick rode swiftly across the heath, with the shouting trio hard at his heels, the scene had a very animated appearance. He crossed the hill—the Hendon Road—passed Crackskull Common—and dashed along the cross-road to Highgate.

Hitherto, no advantage had been gained by the pursuers; they had not lost ground, but still they had not gained an inch, and much spurring was required to maintain their position. But, as they approached Highgate, Dick slackened his pace; and the other party redoubled their efforts. To avoid the town, Dick struck into a narrow path at the right, and rode easily down the hill.

His pursuers were now within a hundred yards, and shouted to him to stand. Pointing to a gate, which seemed to bar their farther progress, Dick unhesitatingly charged it, clearing it in beautiful style. Not so with Coates's party; and the time they lost in unfastening the gate, which none of them liked to leap, enabled Dick to put additional space betwixt them. It did not, however, appear to be his intention altogether to outstrip his pursuers; the chase seemed to give him excitement, which he was willing to prolong as much as was consistent with his safety. Scudding rapidly past Highgate, like a swift-sailing schooner, with three lumbering Indiamen in her wake, Dick now took the lead along a narrow lane that threads the fields in the direction of Hornsey. The shouts of his followers had brought others to join them, and as he neared Crouch End, traversing the lane which takes its name from Du Val, and in which a house frequented by him, stands or stood, " A highwayman—a highwayman!" rang in his ears, in a discordant chorus of many voices.

The whole neighbourhood was alarmed by the cries, and by the tramp of horses—the men of Hornsey rushed into the road to seize the fugitive—and women held up their babes to catch a glimpse of the flying cavalcade, which seemed to gain number and animation as it advanced. Suddenly three horsemen appear in the road; they hear the uproar and the din. "A highwayman—a highwayman!" cry the voices, "stop him—stop him!" But it is no such easy matter. With a pistol in each hand, and his bridle in his teeth, did Turpin boldly pass on. His fierce looks, his furious steed, the impetus with which he pressed forward, bore down all before him. The horsemen gave way, and only served to swell the list of his pursuers.

"We have him now—we have him now!" cried Paterson, exultingly. "Shout for your lives—the turnpike man will hear us—shout again, again—the fellow has heard it—the gate is shut; we have him—ha, ha!"

The old Hornsey toll-bar was a high gate, with *cheveux de frize* in the upper rail; it may be so still. The gate was swung into its lock, and like a tiger in his lair was the prompt custodian of the turnpike trusts ensconced within his doorway, and ready to spring forth upon the run-away. But Dick kept steadily on. He coolly calculated the height of the gate; he looked to the right and to the left; nothing better offered, he spoke a few words of encouragement to Bess, gently patted her neck, then struck spurs into her sides, and cleared the spikes by an inch. Out rushed the amazed turnpike-man, thus unmercifully bilked, and was nearly trampled to death under the feet of Paterson's horse.

"Open the gate, fellow, and be expeditious," shouted the chief constable.

"Not I," said the man, sturdily, "unless I gets my dues. I've been done once already; but strike me stupid if I'm done a second time."

"Don't you perceive that's a highwayman? don't you know that I'm chief constable of Westminster?" said Paterson, showing his staff. "How dare you oppose me in the discharge of my duty?"

"That may be or it may not be," said the man, doggedly; "but you don't pass unless I gets the blunt, and that's the long and short on't."

Amidst a storm of oaths, Coates flung down a crown-piece, and the gate was thrown open.

Turpin took advantage of this delay to breathe his mare; and, striking into a by-lane, at Duckett's green, cantered easily along in the direction of Tottenham. Little repose was allowed him. Yelling like a pack of hounds in full cry, his pursuers were again at his heels. He had now to run the gauntlet of the long straggling town of Tottenham, and various were the devices of the populace to entrap him. The whole place was up in arms, shouting, screaming, running, dancing, and hurling every possible description of missile at the horse and her rider. Dick merrily responded to their clamour, as he flew past, and laughed at the brick-bats that were showered thick as hail, and quite as harmlessly, around him.

A few more miles' hard riding tired the volunteers, and before the chase reached Edmonton, most of them were "*no where.*" Here fresh relays were gathered, and a strong field again mustered. John Gilpin himself could not have excited more astonishment amongst the good folks of Edmonton, than did our Highwayman, as he galloped through their town.

TURPIN'S RIDE TO YORK.

BLACK BESS; OR, THE KNIGHT OF THE ROAD.

Unlike the men of Tottenham, the mob received him with acclamations, thinking, no doubt, that, like " the citizen of famous London town," he rode for a wager. Presently, however, borne on the wings of the blast, came the cries of " Turpin, Dick Turpin !" and the hurrahs were changed to hootings ; but such was the rate at which our Highwayman rode, that no serious opposition could be offered to him. A man in a donkey cart, unable to get out of the way, drew himself up in the middle of the road, but Turpin treated him as he had done the *dub* at the *knapping jigger*, and cleared the driver and his little wain with ease. This was a capital stroke, and well adapted to please the multitude, who are ever taken with a brilliant action. " Hark away, Dick !" resounded on all hands, while hisses were as liberally bestowed upon his pursuers.

CHAPTER IV.

THE SHORT PIPE.

The Peons are capital horsemen, and several times we saw them at a gallop throw the rein on the horse's neck, take from one pocket a bag of loose tobacco, and with a piece of paper, or a leaf of Indian corn, make a cigar, and then take out a flint and steel and light it.
HEAD's *Rough Notes.*

AWAY they fly past scattered cottages, swiftly and skimmingly, like eagles on the wing, along the Enfield-highway. All were well mounted, and the horses, now thoroughly warmed, had got into their paces, and did their work beautifully. None of Coates's party had lost ground, but they maintained it at the expense of their steeds, which were streaming like water carts, while Black Bess had scarcely turned a hair.

" By the mother that bore me," said Titus, as they went along in this slapping style,—Titus, by the by, was on a big, Roman-nosed, powerful horse, well adapted to his weight, but which required a plentiful exercise both of leg and arm, to call forth all his action, and keep his rider along-side his companions—" by the mother that bore me," said he, almost thumping the wind out of his flea-bitten Bucephalus with his calves, after the Irish fashion, " if the fellow isn't lighting his pipe ! I saw the sparks fly on each side of him—and there he goes like a smoky chimney on a frosty morning ! See, he turns his impudent phiz, with the pipe in his mouth ! are we to stand that, Mr. Coates ?"

" Wait awhile, sir—wait awhile," said Coates, " we'll smoke *him*, by and by."

Pæans have been sung in honour of the Peons of the Pampas, by the *Head*long Sir Francis, but what the gallant Major extols so loudly in the South American horsemen, viz. the lighting of a cigar when in mid career, was accomplished with equal ease by our English Highwayman, a hundred years ago, nor was it esteemed by him any extravagant feat either. Flint, steel, and tinder, were bestowed within Dick's ample pouch, the short pipe was at hand, and within a few seconds there was a stream of vapour exhaling from his lips, like the smoke from a steam-boat shooting down the river, and tracking his still rapid course through the air.

"I'll let 'em see what I think of 'em," said Dick, coolly, as he turned his head.

On rush the pack, whipping, spurring, tugging for very life. Again they gave voice, in hopes the waggoner might succeed in stopping the fugitive; but Dick was already by his side. "Harkee, my tulip," cried he, taking the pipe from his mouth as he passed, "tell my friends, behind, they will hear of me at York."

"What did he say?" asked Paterson, coming up the next moment.

"That you'll find him at York," replied the waggoner.

"At York!" echoed Coates, in amaze.

Turpin was now out of sight, and although our trio flogged with might and main, they could never catch a glimpse of him until, within a short distance of Ware, they beheld him at the door of a little public-house, standing with his bridle in his hand, coolly quaffing a tankard of ale. No sooner, however, were they in sight, than Dick vaulted into the saddle, and rode off.

"Devil seize you, sir! why did'nt you stop him?" exclaimed Paterson, as he rode up. "My horse is dead lame. I cannot go any farther. Do you know what a prize you have missed? Do you know who that was?"

"No, sir, I don't," said the publican; "but I know he gave his mare more ale than he took himself, and he has given me a guinea instead of a shilling. He's a regular good un."

"A good un!" said Paterson; "it was Turpin, the famous highway-man. We are in pursuit of him. Have you any horses? our cattle are all blown."

"You'll find the post-house in the town, gentlemen. I'm sorry I can't accommodate you; but I keeps no stabling. I wish you a very good evening, sir." Saying which, the publican retreated to his domicile.

"That's a flash crib, I'll be bound," said Paterson; "I'll chalk you down, my friend, you may rely upon it. Thus far we're done, Mr. Coates; but curse me if I give it in. I'll follow him to the world's end first."

Full of ardour and excitement, determined to execute what he had mentally undertaken, did Turpin hold on his solitary course. Every thing was favourable to his project; the roads were in admirable con-dition, his mare was in like order—she was inured to hard work, had rested sufficiently in town to recover from the fatigue of her recent journey, and had never been in more perfect training. "She has now got her wind in her," said Dick, "I'll see what she can do—hark away, lass—hark away! I wish they could see her now," as he felt her almost fly away with him.

Encouraged by her master's voice and hand, Black Bess started forward at a pace which few horses could have equalled, and scarcely any have sustained so long. Even Dick, accustomed as he was to her magnificent action, felt electrified at the speed with which he was borne along. "Bravo! Bravo!" shouted he, "hark away, Bess!"

The deep and solemn woods through which they were rushing, rang with his shouts, and the sharp rattle of Bess's hoofs; and thus he held his way, while in the words of the ballad,

> Fled past, on right and left, how fast,
> Each forest, grove, and bower;
> On right and left, fled past, how fast,
> Each city, town, and tower.

CHAPTER V.

BLACK BESS.

Dauphin. I will not change my horse with any that treads but on four pasterns. *Ca ha!* He bounds from the earth as if his entrails were hairs; *le cheval volant*, the Pegasus *qui a les narines de feu*! When I bestride him I soar—I am a hawk: the earth sings when he touches it: the basest horn of his hoof is more musical than the pipe of Hermes.
SHAKSPEARE.

BLACK BESS, being undoubtedly the heroine of our tale, our readers will, perhaps, pardon our expatiating a little in this place, upon her birth, parentage, breeding, appearance, and attractions. And first as to her pedigree; for in the horse, unlike the human species, Nature has strongly impressed the noble or ignoble caste; he is the real aristocrat—and the pure blood that flows in the veins of the gallant steed will be infallibly transmitted, if his mate be suitable, throughout all his line. Bess was no *cock tail*—she was thorough bred—she boasted blood in every bright and branching vein:

> If blood can give nobility,
> A noble steed was she;
> Her sire was blood, and blood her dam,
> And all her pedigree.

Behold her paces! how gracefully she moves! She's off!—no eagle on the wing could skim the air more swiftly. Is she not magnificent? Away—away!—the road is level, the path is clear—press on, thou gallant steed, no obstacle is in thy way!—and lo!—the moon breaks forth; her silvery light is thrown over the woody landscape. Dark shadows are cast athwart the road—and the flying figures of thy rider and thyself are traced, like giant phantoms, in the dust!

* * * * * *

"Well," mused Turpin, "I suppose one day it will be with me like all the rest of 'em, and that I shall dance a long lavolta to the music of the four whistling winds, as my betters have done before me; but I trust whenever the chanter culls, and last-speech scribblers get hold of me, they'll at least put no cursed nonsense into my mouth; but make me speak as I have ever felt, like a man who never either feared death, or turned his back upon his friend. In the mean time I'll give them something to talk about. This ride of mine shall ring in their ears long after I'm done for—put to bed with a mattock, and tucked up with a spade:

> And when I am gone, boys, each huntsman shall say,
> None rode like Dick Turpin, so far in a day.

"And thou, too, brave Bess!—thy name shall be linked with mine, and we'll go down to posterity together; and what," added he despondingly, "if it should be too much for thee? what if——but no matter. Better die now, while I am with thee, than fall into the knacker's hands. Better die with all thy honours upon thy head, than drag out thy old age at the sand-cart. Hark forward, lass, hark forward!"

The limits of two shires are already past. They are within the confines of a third. They have entered the merry county of Huntingdon—they have surmounted the gentle hill that slips into Godmanchester. They are by the banks of the rapid Ouse—the bridge is past, and as Turpin rode through the deserted streets of Huntingdon, he heard the eleventh hour given from the iron tongue of St. Mary's spire. In four hours (it was about seven when he had started) Dick had accomplished full sixty miles!

CHAPTER VI.

THE YORK STAGE.

"YORK FOUR DAYS.—*Stage Coach, begins on Friday, the 18th of April,* 1706. All that are desirous to pass from London to York, or from York to London, or any other place on that road, let them repair to the Black Swan, in Holborn, in London, or to the Black Swan, in Coney-street, in York. At both of which places they may be received in a *Stage Coach,* every Monday, Wednesday, and Friday, which performs the whole journey in four days (if God permits), and sets forth at five in the morning. And returns from York to Stamford in two days, and from Stamford, by Huntingdon, in two days more. And the like stages in their return. Allowing each passenger fourteen pounds weight, and all above, threepence per pound. Performed by Benjamin Kingman, Henry Harrison, and Walter Baynes."—*Broadside preserved in the coffee-room of the Black Swan Inn, at York.*

THE night had hitherto been balmy and beautiful, with a bright array of stars, and a golden harvest moon, which seemed to diffuse even warmth with its radiance; but now Turpin was approaching the region of fog and fen, and he began to feel the influence of that dank atmosphere. The intersecting dykes, yawners, gullies, or whatever they are called, began to send forth their steaming vapours, and chilled the soft and wholesome air, obscuring the void, and in some instances, as it were, choking up the

TURPIN'S RIDE TO YORK.

TURPIN STOPPING THE YORK STAGE COACH.

road itself with vapour. But fog or fen was the same to Bess, her hoofs rattled merrily along the road, and she burst from a cloud, like Eöus at the break of dawn.

It was upon this occasion, that travelling through a fog of this kind, the moment they emerged from its dense canopy, they burst upon the York Stage. It was not an uncommon thing for the coach to be stopped; and so furious was the career of our Highwayman, that the man involuntarily drew up his horses. Turpin had also to draw in his rein, a task of no little difficulty, as charging a huge lumbering coach, with its full complement of passengers, was more than even Bess could accomplish. The moon shone bright on Turpin and his mare. He was unmasked, and his features distinctly visible. An exclamation was uttered by a gentleman on the box, who it appeared instantly recognised him.

"Pull up—draw your horses across the road," cried the gentleman; "that's Dick Turpin, the highwayman. His capture would be worth three hundred pounds to you," added he, addressing the coachman, "and is of equal importance to me. Stand!" shouted he, presenting a cocked pistol.

This resolution of the gentleman was not apparently agreeable, either to the coachman or the majority of the passengers, the name of Turpin acting like magic upon them. One man jumped off behind, and was with difficulty afterwards recovered, having tumbled into a deep ditch at the road-side. An old gentleman, with a cotton night-cap, who had popped out his head to swear at the coachman, drew it suddenly in. A faint scream in a female key issued from within, and there was a considerable hubbub on the roof. Amongst other ominous sounds, the guard was heard to click his long horse pistols. "Stop the York four-day stage!" said he, forcing his smoky voice through a world of throat-embracing shawl; "the fastest coach in the kingdom: vos ever sich atrocity heard of? I say, Joe, keep them ere leaders steady—we shall all be in the ditch. Don't you see where the hind wheels are? Who —whoop, I say."

The gentleman on the box now discharged his pistol, and the confusion was redoubled. The white night-cap was popped out like a rabbit's head, and as quickly popped back, on hearing the Highwayman's voice. Owing to the plunging of the horses, the gentleman had missed his aim.

Prepared for such emergencies as the present, and seldom at any time taken aback, Dick received the fire without flinching. He then lashed the horses out of their course, and cantered jauntily by, exclaiming, "A thousand thanks; good night to you, gentlemen."

"Take that with you, and remember the guard," cried the fellow, who, unable to take aim from where he sat, had crept along the coach roof, and discharged from thence one of his large horse pistols at what he took the Highwayman's head, but which, luckily for Dick, was his hat, which he had raised to salute the passengers.

"Remember you," said Dick, coolly replacing his perforated beaver on his brow, " you may rely upon it, my fine fellow, I'll not forget you, the next time we meet."

And off he went like the breath of the whirlwind.

CHAPTER VII.

A ROAD-SIDE INN.

O'er moss and moor, o'er holt and hill,
  His track the steady bloodhounds trace;
O'er moss and moor, unwearied still,
  The furious Earl pursues the chase.
                    THE WILD HUNTSMEN.

EIGHTY and odd miles had now been traversed—the boundary of another county, Northampton, passed; yet no rest, nor respite, had Dick Turpin or his unflinching mare enjoyed. But here he deemed it fitting to make a brief halt.

Bordering the beautiful domains of Burleigh-house, stood a little retired hostelry of some antiquity, which bore the great Lord Treasurer's arms. With this house Dick was not altogether unacquainted. The lad who acted as ostler was known to him. It was now midnight, but a bright and beaming night. To the door of the stable then did he ride, and knocked in a peculiar manner. Reconnoitering Dick through a broken pane of glass in the lintel, and apparently satisfied with his scrutiny, the lad thrust forth a head of hair as full of straw as mad Tom's is represented to be upon the stage. A chuckle of welcome followed his sleepy salutation. " Glad to see you, Captain Turpin," said he; " can I do any thing for you?"

" Get me a couple of bottles of brandy, and a beef-steak," said Dick.

" As to the brandy, you can have that in a jiffy—but the steak, Lord love ye, the old ooman won't stand it at this time; but there's a cold round, mayhap a slice of that might do—or a knuckle of ham?"

" D—n your knuckles, Ralph," cried Dick; " have you any raw meat in the house?"

" Raw meat!" echoed Ralph, in surprise, " oh yes, there's a rare rump of beef—you can have a cut off that if you like."

" That's the thing I want," said Dick, ungirthing his mare; " give me the scraper—there—I can get a whisp of straw from your head—now run and get the brandy—better bring three bottles—uncork 'em, and let me have half a pail of water to mix with the spirit."

" A pail full of brandy and water to wash down a raw steak—my eyes!" exclaimed Ralph, opening wide his sleepy peepers, adding, as he went about the execution of his task, " I always thought them Rumpadders, as they call themselves, rum fellows, but now I'm sartin sure on it."

The most sedulous groom could not have bestowed more attention upon the horse of his heart, than Dick Turpin now paid to his mare. He scraped, chafed, and dried her, sounded each muscle, traced each sinew, pulled her ears, examined the state of her feet, and, ascertaining that "her withers were unwrung," finally washed her from head to foot in the diluted spirit: not, however, before he had conveyed a thimbleful of the liquid to his own parched throat, and replenished what Falstaff calls a "pocket pistol," which he had about him. While Ralph was engaged in rubbing her down after her bath, Dick occupied himself, not in dressing the raw steak in the manner the stable boy had anticipated, but in rolling it round the bit of his bridle.

"She will now go as long as there is breath in her body," said he, putting the flesh-covered iron within her mouth.

The saddle being once more replaced, after champing a moment or two at the bit, Bess began to snort, and paw the earth, as if impatient of delay; and, acquainted as he was with her indomitable spirit and power, her condition was a surprise even to Dick himself. Her vigour seemed inexhaustible, her vivacity was not a whit diminished, but as she was led into the open space, her step was as light and free as when she started on her ride, and her sense of sound as quick as ever. Suddenly she pricked her ears, and uttered a low neigh. A dull tramp was audible.

"Ha!" exclaimed Dick, springing into his saddle, "they come."

"Who come, Captain," asked Ralph.

"The road takes a turn here—don't it?" asked Dick; "sweeps round to the right by the plantations in the hollow?"

"Ay—ay, Captain," answered Ralph, "it's plain you knows the ground."

"What lies behind yon shed?"

"A stiff fence, Captain—a regular rasper; beyond that a hill-side steep as a house; no oss as was ever shoed can go down it."

"Indeed!" laughed Dick.

A loud halloo from Paterson, who seemed advancing on the wings of the wind, told Dick that he was discovered. The Constable was a superb horseman, and took the lead of his party. Striking his spurs deeply into his horse, and giving him bridle enough, he seemed to shoot forward like a shell through the air. The Burleigh Arms retired some hundred yards from the road, the space in front being occupied by a neat garden, with low clipped hedges. No tall timber intervened between Dick and his pursuers, so that the motions of both parties were visible to each other. Dick saw in an instant that if he now started, he should come into collision with his enemies exactly at the angle of the road, and he was by no means desirous of hazarding such a rencontre. He looked wistfully back at the double fence.

"Come into the stable—quick, Captain, quick!" exclaimed Ralph.

"The stable?" echoed Dick, hesitating.

" Ay, the stable—it's your only chance.   Don't you see he's turning the corner, and they are all coming ; quick, sir, quick."

Dick, lowering his head, rode into the tenement, the door of which was most unceremoniously slapped in the Constable's face, and bolted on the other side.

" Villain !" cried Paterson, thundering at the door.   " Come forth— you are now fairly trapped at last—caught like the woodcock, in your own springe.   We have you—open the door I say, and save us the trouble of forcing it.   You cannot escape us.   We will burn the building down, but we will have you."

" What do you want, measter ?" cried Ralph, from the lintel, whence he reconnoitered the Constable, and kept the door fast.   " You're clean mistaken—there be no one here."

" We'll soon see that," and, leaping from his horse, the chief Constable took a short run, to give himself impetus, and with his foot burst open the door.   This being accomplished, he dashed in, but the stable was vacant.   A door was open at the back.   He rushed to it.   The sharply sloping sides of a hill slipped abruptly downwards, within a yard of the door.   It was a perilous descent to the horseman, yet the print of a horse's heels was visible in the dislodged turf, and scattered soil.

" Confusion !" cried the Constable, " he has escaped us.   No !—He is yonder.   See ! he makes again for the road—he clears the fence.   A regular throw he has given us, by the Lord.   No matter ; justice shall be satisfied.   To your steeds, my merry men all.   Hark, and away."

Once more upon the move, Titus forgot his distress, and addressed himself to the attorney, by whose side he rode.

" What place is that we're coming to ?" asked he, pointing to a cluster of moonlit spires belonging to a town which they were rapidly approaching.

" Stamford," replied Coates.

" Stamford !" exclaimed Titus, " by the powers then we've ridden a matter of ninety miles.   Why the great deeds of Redmond O'Hanlon were nothing to this.   I'll remember it to my dying day, with reason," added he, uneasily shifting his position on the saddle.

CHAPTER VIII.

THE GIBBET.

See there, see there, what yonder swings
    And creaks mid whistling rain,
Gibbet and steel—the accursed wheel—
    A murderer in his chain.
                                        WILLIAM AND HELEN.

As the eddying currents sweep over its plains in howling bleak December, did the horse and her rider pass over what remained of Lincoln-

TURPIN'S RIDE TO YORK.

THE GIBBET.

Published by F. Glover, Water Lane, Fleet St.

W. Clark, Lith. 102 High Holborn

shire. Grantham is gone, and now more slowly are they looking up the ascent of Gonerby-hill, a path well known to Turpin; where often, in by-gone nights, had many a purse changed its owner. With that feeling of independence and exhilaration which every one feels, we believe, on having climbed the hill side, Turpin turned to gaze around. There was triumph in his eye, but the triumph was checked as his glance fell upon a gibbet near him to the right, on a round point of hill which is a landmark to the wide vale of Belvoir. Pressed as he was for time, Dick immediately struck out of the road, and approached the spot where it stood. Two scarecrow objects, covered with rags and rusty links of chain, depended from the tree. A night crow screaming around the carcasses, added to the hideous effect of the scene. Nothing but the living highwayman and his skeleton brethren were visible upon the solitary spot. Around him was the lonesome waste of hill, o'erlooking the moonlit valley—beneath his feet, a patch of bare and lightning-blasted sod—above, the wan declining moon and skies, flaked with ghostly clouds—before him, the bleached bodies of the murderers, for such they were.

"Will this be my lot, I marvel?" said Dick, looking upwards, with an involuntary shudder.

"Ay, marry, will it," cried a crouching figure, suddenly springing from beside a tuft of briers that skirted the blasted ground.

Dick started in his saddle, while Bess reared and plunged, at the sight of this unexpected apparition.

"What, ho! thou devil's dam, Barbara, is it thou?" exclaimed Dick, re-assured upon discovering that it was a gipsy queen, and no spectre whom he beheld. "Stand still, Bess—stand, lass. What dost thou here, mother of darkness? Art gathering mandrakes for thy poisonous messes, or pilfering flesh from the dead? Meddle not with their bones, or I will drive thee hence. What dost thou here, I say, old dam of the gibbet?"

"I came to die here!" replied Barbara, in a feeble tone, and, throwing back her hood, she displayed features well nigh as ghastly as those of the skeletons above her.

"Indeed," replied Dick. "You've made choice of a pleasant spot, it must be owned. But you'll not die yet."

"Knowest thou whose these bodies are?" said Barbara, pointing upwards.

"Two of thy race," replied Dick; "right brethren of the blade."

"Two of my sons," cried Barbara; "my twin children. I am come to lay my bones beneath their bones—my sepulchre shall be their sepulchre; my body feed the fowls of the air as their's have fed them. And if ghosts can walk, we'll scour this heath together. I tell thee what, Dick Turpin," said the hag, drawing as near to the Highwayman as Bess would permit her; "dead men walk and ride—ay, ride—there's a comfort for thee. I've seen these do it. I have seen them fling off their chains, and dance—ay, dance with me—with their mother. No revels like dead men's revels, Dick. I shall soon join 'em."

"But you will not lay violent hands upon yourself, mother?" said Dick, with difficulty mastering his terror.

"No," replied Barbara, in an altered tone. "But I will let Nature do her task; would she could do it more quickly, but such a life as mine won't go out without a long struggle. What have I to live for now? Listen to me. I have crawled hither to die. 'Tis five days since I beheld thee, and during that time, food has not passed these lips—nor aught of moisture, save Heaven's dew, cooled this parched throat, nor shall they to the last. That time cannot be far off, and now canst guess how I mean to die? Begone, and leave me, thy presence troubles me. I would breathe my last breath alone, with none to witness the parting pang."

"I will not trouble you more, mother," said Dick, turning his mare, "nor will I ask your blessing."

"My blessing!" scornfully ejaculated Barbara. "Thou shalt have it if thou wilt, but thou wilt find it a curse. Hence!" cried the crone; and as she watched Dick's figure lessening upon the Waste, and at length beheld him finally disappear down the hill-side, she sank to the ground, her frail strength being entirely exhausted.

Long pondering upon this singular interview, Dick pursued his way.

CHAPTER IX.

THE PHANTOM STEED.

I'll speak to thee though hell itself should gape
And bid me hold my peace!

                                        HAMLET.

TIME presses. We may not linger in our course. We must fly on before our flying Highwayman. Full forty miles shall we pass over in a breath. Two more hours have elapsed, and he still urges his headlong career, with heart resolute as ever, and purpose yet unchanged. Fair Newark, and the dashing Trent, "most loved of England's streams," are gathered to his laurels. Broad Notts and its heavy paths, and sweeping glades—its waste (forest no more) of Sherwood past—bold Robin Hood and his merry men, his Marian and his moonlight rides recalled, forgotten, left behind. Hurrah! hurrah! that wild halloo! that waving arm —that enlivening shout. What means it? He is once more upon Yorkshire ground—his horse's hoof beats once more the soil of that noble shire. So transported was Dick, that he could almost have flung himself from the saddle to kiss the dust beneath his feet. Thrice fifty miles has he run, nor has the morn yet dawned upon his labours. Hurrah—the end draws nigh. The goal is in view—halloo, halloo, on!

TURPIN'S RIDE TO YORK.

THE PHANTOM.

Published by F. Glover, Water Lane, Fleet St.

W Clark. lith. N° High Holborn

Bawtrey is past; he takes the lower road by Thorne and Selby. He is skirting the waters of the deep-channelled Don.

Bess now began to manifest some slight symptoms of distress. There was a strain in the carriage of her throat, a dulness in her eye, a laxity in her ear, and a slight stagger in her gait, which Turpin noticed with apprehension. Still she went on, though not at the same gallant pace as heretofore. But as the tired bird still battles with the blast upon the ocean, as the swimmer still stems the stream, though spent, on went she; nor did Turpin dare to check her, fearing that if she stopped she might lose her force, or that if she fell, she would rise no more.

The moon had set. The stars

Pinnacled deep in the intense inane,

had all, save one, the herald of the dawn, withdrawn their lustre, a dull mist lay on the stream, and the air became piercing cold. Turpin's chilled fingers could scarcely grasp the slackening rein, while his eyes, irritated by the keen atmosphere, scarce enabled him to distinguish surrounding objects, or even to guide his steed. It was owing, probably, to this latter circumstance, that Bess suddenly floundered and fell, throwing her master over her head.

Turpin instantly recovered himself. His first thought was for his horse. But Bess was instantly upon her legs—covered with dust and foam, sides and cheeks, and with her large eyes glaring wildly, almost piteously, upon her master.

"Art hurt, lass?" asked Dick, as she shook herself, and slightly shivered. And he proceeded to the horseman's scrutiny. "Nothing but a shake—though that dull eye, those quivering flanks," added he, looking earnestly at her. "She won't go much farther, and I must give it up—what! give up the race just when it's won? No, that can't be. Ha well thought on, I've a bottle of liquid, given me by an old fellow who was a knowing cove, and famous jockey in his day, which he swore would make a horse go as long as he'd a leg to carry him, and bade me keep it for some great occasion. I've never used it, but I'll try it now. It should be in this pocket. Ah! Bess, wench, I fear I'm using thee, after all, as Sir Luke did his mistress, that I thought so like thee—but no matter, it will be a glorious end."

Raising her head upon his shoulder, Dick poured the contents of the bottle down the throat of his mare. Nor had he to wait long before its invigorating effects were instantaneous. The fire was kindled in the glassy orb, her crest was once more erected, her flank ceased to quiver, and she neighed loud and joyously."

"Egad! the old fellow was right," cried Dick. "The drink has worked wonders. What the devil could it have been? It smells like spirit," added he, examining the bottle. "I wish I'd left a taste for myself. But here's that will do as well." And he drained his flask of the last drop of brandy.

Dick's limbs were now become so excessively stiff, that it was with difficulty he could remount his horse; but this necessary preliminary being achieved by the help of a stile, he found no difficulty in resuming his accustomed position upon the saddle. We know not whether there was any likeness between our Turpin and that modern Hercules of the sporting world, Mr. Osbaldeston — far be it from us to institute any similitude, though we cannot help thinking that, in one particular, he resembled that famous "copper-bottomed" Squire. But this we will leave to our readers' discrimination. Dick bore his fatigues wonderfully—he suffered somewhat of that martyrdom which, according to Tom Moore, occurs to "weavers and M.P.'s, from sitting too long"—but again on his courser's back, he cared not for any thing.

Once more at a gallant pace is he traversing the banks of the Don, skirting the fields of flax that bound its sides, and hurrying far more swiftly than its current to its confluence with the Aire. Snaith was past. He was on the road to Selby when dawn first began to break. Here and there a twitter was heard in the hedge; a hare ran across his path, gray looking as the morning self; and the mists began to rise from the earth. A bar of gold was drawn against the east, like the roof of a gorgeous palace; but the mists were heavy in this world of rivers and their tributary streams. The Ouse was before him, the Trent and Aire behind; the Don and Derwent on either hand, all in their way to commingle their currents ere they formed the giant Humber. Amid a region so prodigal of water, no wonder the dews fell thick as rain. Here and there the ground was clear; but then again came a volley of vapour, dim and palpable as smoke.

While involved in one of these fogs, Turpin became aware of another horseman by his side. It was impossible to discern the features of the rider, but his figure in the mist seemed gigantic; neither was the colour of his steed distinguishable. Nothing was visible but the meagre-looking, phantom-like outline of a horse and his rider, and, as the unknown rode upon the turf that edged the way, even the sound of his horse's hoofs were scarce audible. Turpin gazed, not without superstitious awe. Once or twice did he essay to address the strange horseman, but his tongue clove to the roof of his mouth. He fancied he discovered in the mist-exaggerated lineaments of the stranger a wild and fantastic resemblance to his friend Tom King. "It must be Tom," thought Turpin; "he is come to warn me of my approaching end—I will speak to him."

But terror o'ermastered his speech, he could not force out a word, and thus side by side they rode in silence. Quaking with fears he would scarce acknowledge to himself, Dick watched every motion of his companion; he was still, stern, spectre-like, erect, and looked for all the world like a demon on his phantom steed. His courser seemed, in the indistinct outline, to be huge and bony, and as he snorted furiously in the fog, Dick's heated imagination supplied his breath with a due proportion of flame. Not a word was spoken, not a sound heard, save the sullen dead beat of his heels upon the grass. It was intolerable to ride thus cheek by jowl with a goblin. Dick could stand it no longer—he put spurs to his horse, and endeavoured to escape—but it might not be —the stranger, apparently without effort, was still by his side, and Bess's feet, in her master's apprehensions, were nailed to the ground. By and by, however, the atmosphere became clearer—bright quivering beams burst through the vaporous shroud, and then it was, that Dick discovered that the apparition of Tom King was no other than Luke Rookwood. He was mounted on his old horse, Rook, and looked grim and haggard as a ghost vanishing at the crowing of the cock.

"Sir Luke Rookwood, by this light!" exclaimed Dick, in astonishment. Why I took you for——"

"The devil, no doubt?" returned Luke, smiling sternly, "and were sorry to find me so hard pressed; but don't disquiet yourself, I am still flesh and blood."

"Had I taken you for one of mortal mould," said Dick, "you should have soon seen where I'd have put you in the race; but that confounded fog deceived me, and Bess acted the fool as well as myself. However, now I know you, Sir Luke, you must spur alongside, for the hawks are on the wing; and though I've much to say, I've not a second to lose."

*   *   *   *   *   *

In another instant Dick was scouring the plain as rapidly as ever. In the mean time, as Dick has casually alluded to the hawks, it may not be amiss to inquire here how they have flown throughout the night, and whether they are still in chase of their quarry. With the exception of Titus, who was complete done up at Grantham, "having got," as he said, "a complete belly-full of it," they were still on the wing, and resolved sooner or later to pounce upon their prey; pursuing the same system as heretofore, in regard to the post-horses. Paterson took the lead, but the irascible and invincible Attorney was not far in their rear, his wrath having been by no means allayed by the fatigue he had undergone. At Bawtrey they held council of war for a few minutes, being doubtful which course he had taken; but their incertitude was relieved by a foot traveller, who had heard Dick's loud halloo on passing the boundary of Nottinghamshire, and had seen him take the lower road. They struck, therefore, into the path to Thorne, at a hazard, and were soon satisfied they were right. Furiously did they now spur on. They reach Selby; they change horses at the inn in front of the venerable cathedral church; and from the post-boy they learn that a toil-worn horseman, on a jaded steed, had ridden through the town about five minutes before them, and could not be more than a quarter of a mile in advance. "His horse was so dead beat," said the lad, "that I'm sure he cannot have got far; and, if you look sharp, I'll be bound you'll overtake him before he reaches Cawood Ferry."

Mr. Coates was transported. "We'll lodge him snug in York Castle before an hour, Paterson," cried he, rubbing his hands,

"I hope so, sir," said the Chief Constable; "but I begin to have some qualms."

"Now, gentlemen," shouted the post-boy, "come along; I'll soon bring you to him."

CHAPTER X.

CAWOOD FERRY.

The sight renewed my courser's feet
A moment, staggering feebly fleet,
A moment with a faint low neigh
    He answered, and then fell.
With gasps and glazing eyes he lay,
And reeking limbs immoveable,—
His first and last career was done.

MAZEPPA.

THE sun had just o'ertopped the "high eastern hill" as Turpin reached the Ferry of Cawood, and his beams were reflected upon the deep and sluggish waters of the Ouse. Wearily had he dragged his course thither —wearily and slow. The powers of his gallant steed were spent, and he could scarcely keep her from sinking; yet still it was now mid way 'twixt the hours of five and six, nine miles only lay before him, and that thought again revived him. He reached the water's edge; he hailed the ferry-boat, which was then on the other side of the river. At that instant a loud shout smote his ear—it was the halloo of his pursuers. Despair was in his look. He cried to the boatman, and bade him pull fast. The man obeyed, but he had to breast a strong stream, and had a lazy bark and heavy sculls to contend with. He had scarcely left the shore when another shout was raised from the pursuers—the tramp of their steeds grew louder and louder.

The boat had scarcely reached the middle of the stream. His captors were at hand. Quietly did he walk down the bank and as cautiously enter the water. There was a plunge, and steed and rider were swimming down the river.

Seized as it were by a mania for equestrian distinction, Mr. Coates braved the torrent. Not so Paterson. He very coolly took out his bull-dogs, and, watching Turpin, cast up in his own mind the pros and cons of shooting him as he was crossing. "I could certainly hit him," thought or said the constable; "but what of that? A dead highwayman is worth nothing—alive, he weighs £300. I won't shoot him, but I'll make a pretence." And he fired accordingly.

The shot skimmed over the water, but did not, as it was intended, do much mischief. It, however, occasioned a mishap, which had nearly

DEATH OF BLACK BESS.

proved fatal to the aquatic Attorney. Alarmed at the report of the pistol, in the nervous agitation of the moment, Coates drew in his rein so tightly that his steed instantly sank. A moment or two afterwards he rose, shaking his ears, and floundering heavily towards the shore; and such was the chilling effect of this sudden immersion, that Mr. Coates now thought much more of saving himself, than of capturing Turpin. Dick, meanwhile, had reached the opposite bank, and, refreshed by her bath, Bess scrambled up the side of the stream, and speedily regained the road. " I shall do it yet," shouted Dick, " that stream has saved her. Hark away, lass! Hark away!"

Bess heard the cheering cry, and she answered to the call. She roused all her energies—and strained every sinew—put forth all her remaining strength. Once more on wings of swiftness, she bore him away from his pursuers, and Paterson, who had now scrambled on the shore, and made certain of securing him, beheld him spring like a wounded hare from beneath his very hand. " It cannot hold out," said he, " it is but an expiring flash; that gallant steed must soon drop."

" She be regularly booked, that's certain," said the post-boy. " We shall find her on the road."

Contrary to all expectation, however, Bess held on, and set pursuit at defiance. Her pace was swift as when she started, but it was unconscious and mechanical action, it wanted the ease, the lightness, the life of her former riding. She seemed screwed up to a task which she must execute. There was no flogging, no gory heel: but the heart was throbbing, tugging at the sides within, and her spirit spurred her onwards. Her eye was glazing, her chest heaving, her flank quivering, her crest again fallen. Yet she held on. " She is dying, by God!" said Dick. " I feel it——" No, she held on.

Fulford is past. The towers and pinnacles of York burst upon him in all the freshness, the beauty, and the glory of a bright, clear, autumnal morn. The ancient city seemed to smile a welcome, a greeting. The noble Minster and its serene and massive pinnacles, crocketed, lantern-like, and beautiful; St. Mary's lofty spire, All-Hallow's Tower, the massive mouldering walls of the adjacent postern, the grim castle, and Clifford's neighbouring keep—all beamed upon him, " like a bright-eyed face, that laughs out openly." " It is done—it is won," cried Dick. " Hurrah—hurrah!" And the sunny air was cleft with his shouts.

Bess was not insensible to her master's exultation. She neighed feebly in answer to his call, and reeled forwards. It was a piteous sight to see her; to mark her staring, protruding eye-ball—her shaking flanks; but, while life and limb held together, holds she on. Another mile is past. York is near.

" Hurrah!" shouted Dick; but his voice was hushed. Bess tottered —fell. There was a dreadful gasp, a parting moan, a snort, her eye gazed for an instant on her master with a dying glare, then grew glassy, rayless, fixed. A shiver ran through her frame. Her heart had burst.

Dick's eyes were blinded, as with rain. His triumph, though achieved, was forgotten; his present safety unthought of. He stood weeping and swearing like one beside himself.

"And art thou gone, Bess!" cried he in a voice of agony, lifting up his courser's head, and kissing her lips, covered with blood-flecked foam. "Gone, gone! and I have killed the best steed that was ever crossed! And for what?" added Dick, beating his brow with his clenched hand, "for what? for what?"

At that moment the deep bell of the Minster clock tolled out the hour of six.

"I am answered," gasped Dick; "*it was to hear those strokes!*"

Turpin was roused from the state of stupefaction into which he had fallen by a smart slap on the shoulder. Recalled to himself by the blow, he started at once to his feet, while his hands sought his pistols, but he was spared the necessity of using them by discovering in the intruder the bearded visage of a gipsy, habited in mendicant weeds, and sustaining a large wallet upon his shoulders.

"So, it's all over with the best mare in England, I see," said the gipsy, to whom Turpin was well known; "but I can guess how it has happened; you are pursued."

"I am," said Dick, roughly.

"Your pursuers are at hand?"

"Within a few hundred yards."

"Then why stay here? fly while you can."

"Never, never," cried Turpin; "I'll fight it out here, by Bess's side. Poor lass! I've killed her—but she has done it—ha, ha!—we have won —what?" and his utterance was again choked.

"Hark! I hear the tramp of horse, and shouts," cried the gipsy. "Take this wallet, you will find a change of dress within it; dart into that thick copse; save yourself."

"But Bess, I cannot leave her," exclaimed Dick, with an agonising look at his horse.

"And what died Bess for, but to save you?" rejoined his friend.

"True, true," said Dick; "but take care of her. Don't let those dogs of hell meddle with her carcase."

"Away," cried the man; "leave Bess to me."

Possessing himself of the wallet, Dick disappeared in the adjoining copse.

He had not been gone many seconds, when the pursuers rode up.

"Who is this?" exclaimed Paterson, flinging himself from his horse; "this is not Turpin."

"Certainly not," replied the gipsy, coolly. "I am not exactly the figure for a highwayman."

"Where is he? what has become of him?" asked Coates in despair.

"Escaped, I fear," replied Paterson. "Have you seen any one, fellow?"

"I have seen no one," replied the gipsy. "I am but this instant arrived; this dead horse lying in the road attracted my attention."

"Ha!" exclaimed Paterson, "this may be Turpin after all. He has as many disguises as the devil himself, and may have carried that goat's hair in his pocket." Saying which he seized the old man by the beard, and shook it with as little reverence as the Gaul handled the chin of the Roman senator.

"The devil! hands off," roared the gipsy. "By Salmon, but I shan't stand such usage. Do you think a beard like mine is the growth of a few minutes? Hands off, I say."

"Regularly done!" said Paterson, removing his hold, and looking as blank as a cartridge.

"Ay," exclaimed Coates, "all owing to this worthless piece of carrion. If it were not that I hope to see him dangling from those walls," pointing towards the Castle, "I should wish her master were by her side now. To the dogs with her;" and he was about to spurn the breathless carcase of poor Bess, when a sudden blow, dealt by the gipsy's staff, felled him to the ground.

"I'll teach you to molest me," said the angry old man, about to attack Paterson.

"Come, come," said the discomfited Chief Constable, "no more of this. It's plain we're in the wrong box. Every bone in my body aches sufficiently without the aid of your cudgel, old fellow. Come, Mr. Coates, take my arm, and let's be moving. We've had an infernal long ride for nothing."

"Not so," replied Coates; "I've paid pretty dearly for it. However, let us see if we can get any breakfast at the bowling-green, yonder; though I have already had my morning draught," added the facetious man of law, looking at his dripping apparel.

"Poor Black Bess!" said Paterson, wistfully regarding the body of the mare as it lay stretched at his feet. "Thou deservedst a better fate, and a better master. In thee Turpin has lost his best friend. Light be the ground over thee, thou wonder-working mare!"

To the bowling-green the party proceeded, leaving the old gipsy in undisturbed possession of the lifeless body of Black Bess. Paterson ordered a substantial repast to be prepared with all possible expedition.

A countryman in a smock was busily engaged at his morning's meal.

"To see that fellow bolt down his breakfast, one would think he had fasted for a month," said Coates; "see the wholesome effects of an honest, industrious life, Paterson. I envy him his appetite; I should fall to with more zest were Dick Turpin in his place."

The countryman looked up. He was an odd-looking fellow, with a terrible squint, and a strange contorted countenance.

"An ugly dog!" exclaimed Paterson; "what a devil of a twist he has got!"

I

"What's that you says about Dick Taarpin?" asked the countryman, with his mouth half full of bread.

"Have you seen aught of him?" asked Coates.

"Not I," mumbled the rustic; "but I hears aw the folk hereabouts talk on him; they say he sets all the lawyers and constables at defiance, and laughs in his sleeve at their efforts to catch him—ha, ha! He gets over more ground in a day than they do in a week—ho, ho!"

"That's all over now," said Coates, peevishly. "He has cut his own throat—ridden his famous mare to death."

The countryman almost choked himself, in the attempt to bolt a huge mouthful. "Ay—indeed! How happened that?" asked he, so soon as he recovered speech.

"The fool rode her from London to York, last night," returned Coates; "such a feat was never performed before; what horse could be expected to live through such work as that?"

"Ah, he were a fool to attempt that," observed the countryman, "but you followed belike?"

"We did."

"And took him arter all?" asked the rustic, squinting more horribly than ever.

"No," returned Coates, "I can't say we did. But we'll have him yet. I'm pretty sure he can't be far off—we may be nearer him than we imagine."

"May be so, sir," returned the countryman; "but might I be so bold as to ask how many horses you used i' the chase; some half dozen, perhaps?"

"Half dozen!" growled Paterson; "we had twenty at the least."

"And I ONE," mentally ejaculated Turpin, for he was the countryman.

END OF TURPIN'S RIDE TO YORK.

J. Cunningham, Printer, Crown-court, Fleet-street